Hello Kitty®

Visits Grandma!

Written by Elizabeth Smith
Illustrated by Jean Hirashima

HARRY N. ABRAMS, INC., PUBLISHERS

Hello Kitty loves spending the weekend with Grandma White.
Grandma White always thinks of such fun things to do!

Saturday morning they paint landscapes outside. Grandma White teaches Hello Kitty how to mix a pale sky blue.

After painting, they eat their picnic lunch. When they are finished, they look up into the clouds. Hello Kitty sees a dog and a rabbit. Grandma White sees an elephant!

"Grandma White, you have such a good imagination!" exclaims Hello Kitty.

Grandma White loves to do embroidery. On Saturday evening, she teaches Hello Kitty many different kinds of stitches: French knots, lazy daisies, and chain stitches.

Hello Kitty is making a sampler of everything she has learned!

Sunday morning, Grandma White shows Hello Kitty how to make triple-layer pudding cake. Hello Kitty sifts the flour and adds the chocolate. After mixing the batter, Grandma White pours it into the cake pans. Grandpa White shows up just in time to help them lick the bowl. All three agree, "This batter is delicious!"

While the cake is baking, Hello Kitty plays dress-up. She picks out the shiniest shoes and the prettiest pink dress from Grandma White's closet.

"Why, how stylish you look!" says Grandma White.

In Grandma White's dresser drawer, Hello Kitty finds a bunch of old photos.

"Grandma White, did you really do that?" she asks eagerly. "How brave you are!"

Grandma White tells
Hello Kitty all about
her great adventures.

When the cake is done, Grandma White and Hello Kitty decorate it with sunflowers and roses made out of frosting.
"I have an idea," says Grandma White. "Let's dress up and have a tea party!"

They both put on flowery dresses and sit in Grandma White's dining room. Before they eat their cake and drink their tea,

Hello Kitty politely asks, "Grandma White, would you like one lump of sugar or two?"

Late Sunday afternoon, they make popcorn and watch one of Grandma White's favorite movies—a romantic comedy. They agree the hero of the story is very handsome indeed!

The weekend goes by too quickly. "Come again," says Grandma White as Hello Kitty heads home. "Whenever you visit, I have so much fun!"

Illustrations by Jean Hirashima
Text by Elizabeth Smith

Design by Celina Carvalho
Production Manager: Jonathan Lopes

Library of Congress Cataloging-in-Publication Data

Smith, Elizabeth, 1965-
Hello Kitty visits Grandma / Elizabeth Smith ; illustrated by Jean Hirashima.
p. cm.
Summary: Hello Kitty spends a weekend doing all sorts of fun things with her Grandma White,
including painting and baking a special cake.
ISBN 0-8109-4937-7 (alk. paper)
[1. Cats—Fiction. 2. Grandmothers—Fiction.] I. Hirashima, Jean, ill. II. Title.

PZ7.S64498Hen 2004
[E]—dc22
2004000871

Printed and bound in China
10 9 8 7 6 5 4 3 2 1

Harry N. Abrams, Inc.
100 Fifth Avenue
New York, NY 10011
www.abramsbooks.com

Abrams is a subsidiary of